PETA

AN ELEMENTAL SERIES NOVELLA

SHANNON MAYER

For my readers, and my sweet soul kitty, Falene.

Peta
A Companion Novella to "Firestorm"

1

Loam's death should have been hard for me. I should have grieved before reporting back to the mother goddess. Yet I found it hard to grieve for a charge who'd never truly wanted me in his life, and had made that clear on a daily basis. To him, I was more of an embarrassment than anything else. I snorted softly.

"Twelve. Perhaps that is my lucky number and I will finally be done traipsing after fire elementals who are so prideful they can't even see when they are walking into danger." My feet sank into the snow all the way to my belly. I shifted from my housecat form to snow leopard and bounded up the steep slope. According to humans, the mountain was haunted by those who'd died in an attempt to ascend it. I'd never seen a ghost though, in all the times I'd climbed to the mother goddess to speak with her. The snow swirled in tight little circles in front of my nose, and then shifted and turned into a hand that beckoned me forward.

So the mother goddess knew I was here. I wasn't surprised.

Leaping onto a rock ledge, I pulled myself to the front

doorstep of the mother goddess. Curled in a tight circle on the bare rock, her form was that of my own mother, a clouded snow leopard. Her dark spots were perfectly laid out over her pale cream fur, and her pristine blue eyes were vibrant against the snowy backdrop. Her large, rounded ears twitched toward me.

I went to my belly and bowed my head, breathing in the scent of the earth and ice. "Mother."

"Child, you have not had time to grieve. Why do you come so quickly to me?" Her voice held only the slightest rebuke.

I kept my head down. "I wish to be set free of my charges. I have overseen the lives of a dozen of your elemental children. More than any other familiar in your care. Please. Set me free."

She moved toward me, laying against my side and placing her head across my back. "You believe it is freedom you seek?"

"It is." I lifted my head. "You know that is my heart's desire."

"I know your heart, Nepeta. I know it better than you know yourself, I think." She started to purr, the soft rumble soothing along my back and I closed my eyes. This time she would allow me to go my own way. To live out a natural life no longer tied to an elemental who wouldn't listen to me regardless of how right I was.

"One last charge, Nepeta. One final life to watch over. Will you do that?"

She asked, as if I had a choice. I'd heard of familiars turning her down, but I could not be that one. The mother goddess called me to her and I would always answer her as I should.

A sigh slipped out of me. "Yes, I will. What Salamander do you have in mind this time?"

The thought crossed my mind that she could assign me to Fiametta. After all, we knew that Jag, Fiametta's current familiar was barely even allowed to be in the throne room. I kept my mouth shut; the last thing I wanted was to be stuck with the queen.

"Larkspur. That is who you will guide."

"Larkspur?" The name was familiar, but not a Salamander name at all. A flower, known for its beauty and deadly poison. An image of the Deep flowed over my mind, of diving into the water and fighting to keep a Terraling alive.

"You mean Dirt Girl?" The words screeched out of me as I stood. "A Terraling? You've got to be joking. Their familiars are *canines*."

The mother goddess stared at me, her eyes unfathomable in their serenity. "I do not joke about things of this nature, child of mine. She is in terrible need of your help. And there is no other familiar I would assign to her."

"Why, because you want her to die with the bad luck cat?" I bit the words out, knowing I was being irrational and more than a little disrespectful. But a Terraling? They were weak and useless. I couldn't understand why the mother goddess would assign me to one. Unless she thought the same of me.

My heart sank and I turned my face away.

"Child, that is not why I give you to her. She is as special to me as you are special to me. Trust that I would not assign you to someone who wouldn't be—"

"Loam hated me. So did the one before him, and the one before that. Do you know how long its been since any of my charges even listened to me? They draw strength from me without thought, they ignore my advice and treat me as if I am lower than them. None of them, except for my first, has even shared a meal with me."

The mother goddess padded forward and butted her head against mine. "I know all this, and I know that it tears at your heart. Yet you learned from all of them, Nepeta. You learned and you gained what you would need for this moment. I know it was hard and I wept when they didn't love you as they should. It was all preparation for this time in your life."

My eyes blurred with her words. "Then why this? A final insult?"

"A final charge, Nepeta. There will be no more after this. Larkspur will be your last. That is my promise to you."

A sigh slipped out of me. "Then I am off to the Rim. Perhaps a change of scenery will not be so bad. Is Griffin still there? Would you like me to take him a message?"

"No, my consort and I are not on speaking terms right now." She grimaced. "Besides, you are not going to the Rim."

I tipped my head to one side. "Is she still in the Deep?" I didn't like the world of the Undines, but I would go there if that was where my charge was. Duty was something I understood far too well.

"No, Larkspur is in the Pit. And she has landed herself in some rather hot water."

I twitched my tail but otherwise kept my thoughts to myself. Of course Dirt Girl had landed herself in trouble. How was I not surprised?

The mother goddess licked the side of my face. "Let your heart guide you, Nepeta. That is the only way you both will survive this."

I stared at her. "She cannot be more dangerous to my

health than Loam was. He was a fool and all but allowed the Undines to manipulate him."

The mother goddess's eyes filled my vision as the icy cold swirled through my fur and I was sped away to my newest charge. "She is far more dangerous than Loam, Nepeta, both to herself and to the world. It is why she needs you."

I opened my mouth to ask one last question, but it was swept away in the swirl of snow melting into water, cold sliding into crushing heat, and my freedom turned into the chains of yet another charge.

2

The Pit was as it always had been. Hotter than hell and layered with intrigue as Fiametta tried to ferret out the firewyrms without letting onto the masses that was what she was doing. But that was no longer a concern of mine, tied as I was to a Terraling.

My lip curled up at the very thought. Already I could feel the growing bond between Dirt Girl and me. I fought it, stuffing it to the back of my head. I wasn't about to get all tied up in emotions like a first time familiar. It had been years since I'd let a charge truly in; not that any of them had wanted a true bond with me.

There would be no friendship here between myself and the Terraling. This was a job, and when it was done, I would finally be free to go.

Free to live my own life and maybe even have a litter of my own kittens. I thought about that for a moment before dismissing it. Who was I kidding? I'd been mothering elementals for hundreds of years. What need did I have for mothering more creatures who wouldn't listen to me?

None.

I followed the ties that drew me closer to the Dirt Girl, and ended up in the healer's rooms. The Terraling lay on the bed and Brand held her down while Smit put her shoulder back into its socket. Within seconds the pain that coursed through her whispered along my spine; a shadow of what she felt. I could take the pain from her, but I didn't. Whatever trouble she'd been in before I arrived had nothing to do with me.

She could suffer for all I cared.

In my housecat form, I was easily missed and I sat on the edges, watching her interact with Brand and the healer. Or at least, I thought I'd been incognito.

Smit let out a laugh. "What are you doing here, Peta? I thought the queen had you banished."

I glared at him as shame burned me all the way to the tips of my fur. I couldn't even answer him. Not really. The queen hadn't banished me, but the rumor had begun to circulate when Fiametta had publicly wondered why all my charges died. If perhaps she *should* banish me to save her people. That had been all it took for people to believe I'd been kicked out. That and being stuck with Loam in the Deep for as long as I was did not help the rumor.

Looking up at the Dirt Girl, I stared into her eyes. One green, the other gold. They marked her for what she was. A half-breed. Weak and useless.

Just like me.

"Hello, Peta." She slid to the side of her bed leaving room for me to leap up, but I didn't want to touch her. I stared at her, wondering what in my nine lives the mother goddess was thinking.

"Dirt Girl. I see you're in trouble again."

Brand grunted. "Cat, you're pretty damn mouthy for one on the edge of being booted out."

I let out a sneeze and wiped a paw over my face. "Please. It's is not my fault I've always been assigned to idiots."

Dirt Girl dropped her feet to the floor. "Good luck with your next fire assignment then. I hope they are smarter than your last."

She started to walk away from me and I grabbed her with my claws, digging into the first layer of her calves. Enough to get her attention. Dirt Girl stopped and looked down at me, an eyebrow arched over her green eye. I didn't like that her green eye was so like mine in coloring. Maybe I was supposed to be with her.

No. No. No. I was doing this for one reason only. The mother goddess asked. I refused to get my heart involved with this charge. I had to believe she would make it easy for me to keep her at a tail's length. Stupid, useless, weak. My entire life with Salamanders had informed me of those truths. So that would make it easy to not get attached.

"What do you want, cat?"

I let go of her, but didn't break eye contact.

"Dirt Girl, I'm going to need that luck. The mother goddess has given me my new assignment already and I don't like it."

She threw an arm into the air. "Wonderful. Good luck. I have to go, things to do." With that she strode away.

Luck. I was quite sure I was going to need more than luck to get through this assignment.

Brand led the Dirt Girl away and I hurried after them while trying not to look like I was hurrying.

"Bad luck cat," Smit said and I fought the cringe that curled down my shoulders.

"What?"

"*Did* you get reassigned yet?" There was laughter in his voice; yet again I was the butt of a joke.

If I told them I'd been reassigned to the Dirt Girl, how much worse would the laughter be?

"No." I spit the word out and trotted from the room, following the ties that bound me to the Terraling. Gah. Who would willingly live in a dirty, noisy forest? The Pit was hot, but always clean. Of course, if I had a choice, I'd be living in the mountains, deep in the snow where I never had to worry about another elemental being stupid and trying to keep them alive only to watch them die.

I followed Dirt Girl to the stairs that led down into the living quarters. Maybe I could look after her at a distance.

No, child. You must be with her. Trust me. And trust her. She is not like the others.

"We'll see about that," I muttered to myself. I drew in a breath and let out a meow.

Brand looked back first and let out a loud snort. "We don't need you following us, bad luck cat."

I leapt from the top of the stairs straight for the Terraling, aiming for the shoulder that had recently been put back together. Perhaps it wasn't very nice, but I didn't like Terralings. Not even one I'd been assigned to. I landed easily, feeling her fight not to drop away from me.

Balancing easily, I made myself comfortable ignoring her twinge of pain. Time to spit out why I was following her. The words were like rancid meat on my tongue. "I told you I had a new assignment." I stared hard into her eyes, willing her to understand.

She lifted her hands and sputtered. "No, you're kidding me, right? I don't need a familiar."

I doubted she didn't need a familiar, but all I heard was she didn't want me. Exactly like the others. The realization shouldn't have hurt, but it did. Even a Terraling dirt grubber didn't want me.

The Terraling shook her head. "Peta, you must be mistaken. You're meant for a Salamander. Not . . . me."

I draped myself across her shoulders and twitched my tail down the front of her neck. It sure as hell wasn't like I'd wanted to be her familiar. "I didn't ask for this. If you have a complaint, get in line to take it up with the mother goddess."

Brand stared at us with wide eyes. "I'd get in line. That cat has lost more of her charges than any familiar in the Pit. Seriously, that cat is bad luck."

Damn him.

She lifted a hand and brushed it along my back, like a child touching something breakable for the first time. Something of value even. The shiver that ran through me was very light, but I felt it from the tip of my tail to the tip of my nose.

"She saved me twice already, Brand. If the mother goddess feels I am deserving of her then I am grateful."

Her words . . . the respect in her voice brought tears to my eyes and I closed them. No tears, no more tears. Not for any elemental. They didn't deserve it. But maybe . . .no, I would not fall for this. Her words were just words, they meant nothing.

When the time came, she would throw me under the lava flow like every other charge I'd had.

As we walked, Brand spoke to Dirt Girl about the situation and I added what I could, as helping her was my task. Not that I expected her to listen to my advice.

Her friend Ash had been thrown in the dungeon and was to be executed in a matter of days for crimes she had committed. Unless Dirt Girl could find a way for him to be exonerated, he would die in place of her.

What caught me off guard though was the pain in Dirt

Girl when she learned more about the men she'd killed, of the women and families they'd left behind. It stunned me.

How long had it been since I'd had a charge who felt the consequences of their actions?

Not since the first and even he had let his pride get the better of him in the end, believing he was capable of taking on more than he truly could.

I butted my head against her ear, to get her attention. "You do what you must to survive. We all do, Dirt Girl. That you feel their loss . . . that is good. When you stop feeling the pain of your actions . . .that is when you must be afraid. When you no longer care if you kill, then we have a problem."

Slowly she straightened. "Take me to her." Her, the pregnant wife of one of the Enders killed. Not a good idea; but I kept my mouth shut. If Dirt Girl wanted to get her ass handed to her, far be it from me to interfere.

Brand shook his head. "No. She is crazed with her loss."

Under me, the Terraling opened herself to her power and I fought not to let my jaw drop. The sensation was that of the mountain sitting up and listening to her, waiting to be commanded.

So much for being weak and useless.

She lifted a hand and touched one of my front paws. "Peta. Do you know where she is?"

I assumed she still meant the wife of the one Ender, the wife who was pregnant.

"Brand is right. Now is not the time. Later perhaps," I said, fully expecting her to ignore me.

She paused, breathing slowly. "All right, Peta."

"You're listening to me?" Shock filtered through me, like lightning on a dry summer night.

"That is part of your job, isn't it? To advise me?"

"Yes, but . . . rarely does anyone abide by their familiars. It's why so few of us are connected to elementals now. Even the queen discounts Jag."

I snapped my mouth shut. I'd said too much. Despite the fact I was now Dirt Girl's familiar, my home had been the Pit for most of my life. My loyalty was to Fiametta, even if she was a hard ass.

Brand led the rest of the way to his home, and I mulled over what had happened as they sat at the dinner table. It had to be a fluke. There was no reason for her to trust me, or listen to me.

Very likely she'd done it for show because Brand had been watching.

Yet, I couldn't help but feel her emotions as they skimmed through her body. Gratitude. She was grateful I was with her.

I kept my mouth closed and my jaw tight. I would not feel for this Terraling. I would not.

Brand and his wife Smoke fed Dirt Girl while I sat on her shoulder. They ignored me as if I were an inanimate object. No doubt they thought I truly was bad luck and if they ignored me they would stay safe.

Breathing evenly, I kept the hurt at bay. It should not have been a surprise to me, yet still the snub bit at what was left of my pride. I withdrew further into myself and away from the conversation.

Until the Terraling offered me her cup of milk, shocking me out of at least one of my nine lives.

Mother goddess . . . I could not turn it down. I ducked my head into the stone cup and lapped up the cool, frothy milk as a tear slipped out of one eye and into the drink.

"How long has it been, Peta, since one of your charges actually accepted you?" Smoke asked.

I pulled my head out, milk clinging to my whiskers in tiny white droplets at the very ends. I did not answer Smoke. "That is enough for me, Dirt Girl."

Dirt Girl gave me the most imperceptible of nods and then drank the rest of the milk down in a gulp.

No idea . . .she had no idea what she'd done. Sharing with me like that, it was a formal acknowledgment that I was her familiar and that she would work with me as a teammate. Putting my needs and knowledge on par with her own.

Could I trust it, though?

That was the question I had no answer to, and the one that scared me the most. Trust.

Could I trust her with my heart?

No. I would not trust her. She may have shared her drink with me, but I doubted she even understood what it meant. I let a slow breath slip out of me. So it meant nothing to her.

And I would let it mean nothing to me.

3

Smoke took the Terraling down to wash clothes so they could discuss the problems within the Pit without Fiametta's spies overhearing. Dirt Girl actually washed clothes while she talked, and I was perhaps a little bit proud of her. Perhaps. At least she was helping while she sought answers. There was no way she could know Smoke struggled with her health. The fire half-breed should've known by staying in the Pit she'd suffer as her body craved the windswept mountains of the Eyrie. Still she never left and it weakened her.

I sat in the now empty basket, studying my charge asking about the fire elementals. It was almost like she *wanted* to know more about someone besides her people.

"There is more," I said, jumping into the conversation. "Something with the night bells has shifted. People are sleeping longer, and are harder to wake up. I have seen that, too."

Dirt Girl turned her face to me, her mouth opening as if she would speak, and then she dove into the rushing water.

I leapt out of the basket and ran to the edge, but the

Terraling was already swept down river toward the lava flows that warmed the water.

Shifting into my leopard form, I sprinted along the edge to catch up with her. What was she doing diving into the water like that? Was she crazy?

Finally she broke the surface, but she was closing in on the lava. A Salamander I wouldn't even have gone after, but the Terraling wouldn't survive the excessive temperature.

"Dirt Girl, swim to the edge and don't dawdle."

Her eyes met mine and I saw the heat behind them, how it was sucking her down and sapping her strength. "I'm sorry," she whispered and the pain that flowed between us was not pain of the body.

Pain of the heart.

Damn her, I liked her too much already to let her die.

The water pushed her toward me and with a snarl I lashed out, digging my claws into her arm and yanking her close enough that I could get my mouth on her other hand and drag her out of the water.

"Dirt Girl. If you decide to go swimming, perhaps a less dangerous place would be good, eh?" I paced by her head, my heart stumbling over what had almost happened. I'd almost failed her. No. I would not feel that worry again. I would not care that her death would matter. "Is it not enough everyone thinks I'm bad luck? To lose you on the first day I'm assigned to you would be the end of my reputation completely. How could I ever show my face again?"

That was not the truth though; the truth was far more upsetting. I'd liked her since I met her in the Deep. She'd defended me against Loam's insults and those few kind words had stuck with me.

She lifted her hand. "Thanks for saving me. That's three times now. You must like me."

Indeed. That's what I was trying to avoid.

I pushed my life energy toward her, giving her enough that her hands would heal, that the burns over the skin would disappear. Fatigue swept over me, but I was used to it and I ignored it.

That was the price of being a familiar. Losing a piece of yourself on a regular basis to your charge.

"What are you doing?" She frowned up at me, her two toned eyes glittering like the jewels in the queen's throne room.

"I'm letting you draw on me. That is what elementals do; they allow their charges to be stronger, faster, and heal at a speed that keeps them alive. Or is supposed to, anyway."

She frowned harder. "Well, stop it. I don't want to draw from you."

"Too good to draw from a cat?" I spit out, turning my face away from her as Smoke approached.

Even the Terraling didn't want me.

That stung.

Smoke helped the Terraling and within moments there was more trouble with the pregnant wife of the Ender Lark killed storming toward us with a group of women.

But it was the way Dirt Girl handled the grieving woman . . . the kindness and the way she took responsibility for her actions that surprised me. Almost as if she truly cared that what she'd done had caused others pain.

And then she used Spirit.

Not since I was a young cat had I felt Spirit and the familiarity of it soothed some of my fears. The Terraling used Spirit quietly, gently, as if it were to be respected and feared.

Smart girl. Even if she was a dirt girl. Her use of Spirit helped me understand a little more about her. The moments of almost connecting with her was because my first charge had been a Spirit Walker.

So it had nothing to do with her personally the moments of feeling close. More of a matter of the past coming back to haunt me.

After dealing with the women, we went to Cactus's home. Though I doubted he could be of any help to us. He was too tied into the queen and her machinations; I questioned if he would even speak to us.

So when the prick opened his door and we stepped in . . . I was shocked on more than one level.

And then very, very afraid; what Cactus had in his home was bordering on treason.

The greenery that sprouted from every nook of stone was lush and beautiful. Every shade of green I'd ever seen in my life from the deepest of hues that seemed nearly black to the palest of tones that could almost be called cream and everything in between. Added into that were the heavy hanging fruits and flowers scattered everywhere, like explosions of color. The air was cleaner, cooler, and soothed my senses in every way possible. I leapt from Dirt Girl's shoulder to the ground. Even the rock below my feet was covered in a thick moss that beckoned me to lie down and roll around with abandon.

"Dirt Girl, is your home like this?"

"Parts of it."

"I could handle being your familiar if this is what my paws get to be on." I kneaded the ground, my eyelids fluttering. I tipped my face up in time to see the prick plant his lips on Dirt Girl's.

Mouse turds, this could be trouble. The prick was known to be a flirt, and the reputation that floated with him was that he was happy to bed anything that moved. Though

I had no actual bearing that the rumors were true, I had no reason to doubt them.

"Peta," Dirt Girl scooped me up so we were eye to eye. "Are you really with me? Can I trust you with my life?"

I frowned. Why would she ask me that? Did she think so little of me that I would turn on her? "The mother goddess assigned me to you herself. It is my job to help you stay alive."

"That's not what I'm asking." She paused and I could almost see the thoughts rolling through her. "Peta, are you *with* me?"

Her emotions swelled, and I pushed at them, keeping myself from truly feeling what she was.

"You're going to be the death of all nine of my lives, aren't you?"

"I hope not."

I snorted and twitched my ears. "I am with you, Dirt Girl. What are you going to ask of me?"

"Can you get into the Ender Barracks? There is an Ender with a scar on the top of his right hand. I need to know his name."

I leapt from her hands, bracing myself. Now I had to decide. Would I help her truly or stay loyal to the only home I'd truly known? "What does the scar look like?"

She crouched beside me and turned her hand palm down. The scars on her hand from me grabbing her with my mouth had faded to silvery lines. "Like my scars only thicker, like a bigger cat maybe clawed him."

I suspected which Ender she spoke of. Coal had been the idiot to challenge Damascus, the Bengal tiger assigned to the queen's son, Flint. Yet I didn't tell her his name, and a prickle of guilt nipped at my toes. No, I was being loyal to my people. Coal may or may not have been the problem anyway. There was no point in ratting him out. "He should be easy to find. Why do you want him?"

"He's a traitor to the queen. If we give him to her, I think we should be able to bargain for Ash's life," she said. Cactus gave a low grunt.

"You do not know her very well then."

Again, she looked to me. "And what do you think, cat? You think the queen will not bargain?"

"Cactus is right. She won't bargain." I shook my head, ears twitching. "But it might buy us time if you offer her a traitor on a platter. She likes nothing more than to wield the Lava Whip herself on those she deems deserving of punishment."

A shiver ran though Dirt Girl. She was right to be afraid. The Lava Whip would kill anyone who wasn't a Salamander, and the death would be brutally painful. I'd seen it only once, and that was enough to give me nightmares.

"Time is better than nothing," she said softly. "See if you can find the Ender I described to you. But be careful."

Her worry over me came through the bonds loud and clear. I bobbed my head and ran down the hallway, my footsteps eaten by the moss, ignoring the warm glow her worry lit in me.

Through the tunnels I trotted, and all around me were those who'd known me for years.

"Bad luck cat, get outta here."

"Kill anyone lately?"

"Goddess, why's she still around?"

They were just words, but they hurt as if they were sharp sticks jabbed against my heart.

Hadn't I done enough? I had asked the mother goddess that very thing. Was it not enough that I'd suffered through losing twelve charges? Most familiars stayed with one, maybe two of those they were set to watch over. Twelve.

Twelve lives.

Twelve deaths.

Twelve times I'd failed my task to make sure they outlived me.

And that was why I had tried to save Dirt Girl in the Deep. I saw in her a strength I had a hard time admitting even to myself.

She was a survivor, a fighter for those who needed her.

But would she survive me and my bad luck? Even I could admit my track record was less than stellar.

The image of her going under the water, her blond hair sucked down and her eyes closing slammed into me like a runaway avalanche.

One day of bonding, and the thought of losing her shook me to the core. Trembling, I stumbled into the Enders barracks. It was empty, not a single Ender walked through the training room.

Breathing hard I searched through the various rooms, looking for Coal while my mind raced. At least I would be able to tell her the truth; the Ender she sought was nowhere to be found.

Dirt Girl could not know how my feelings for her were growing stronger. She would use me, and leave me out on a spindly dead branch to fall from when I needed her most.

With that firmly in mind, I headed back to the prick's house. Curled up like children in the forest, the two of them were wrapped around each other. The innocence of how they lay struck me.

Indeed, they were like children. Neither had even seen their first century yet, while I'd seen two and a half. If she wasn't careful, I doubted she ever *would* see her first century.

I leapt up onto the bed, and she opened her eyes. I held her gaze, hoping she couldn't see the truth behind my words.

"The Ender you're looking for is nowhere to be found, Dirt Girl." I pushed myself under her jaw, curling into the space between her chest and chin so I could rest my head in the crook of her neck. I yawned. "Perhaps he is one of the Enders you killed."

I knew he wasn't but I didn't want her to go against Coal. He was tough, even for an Ender. An idiot to be sure, but still very tough.

The last time that someone challenged him, he'd broken their back and then thrown them into the lava. I did not want that for the Terraling.

I'd been hoping we would sleep awhile, but Dirt Girl stood, holding me tightly to her chest.

Prick swatted her ass.

"Keep your hands to yourself, Prick," I snapped, feeling more than a little protective. The last thing Dirt Girl needed was to get her heart messed with by him.

I bared my teeth at him to make sure he got the point. No one touched my charge unless she was okay with it. Even if I wasn't sure of her, I knew my job and what it entailed.

As we walked, heading for Brand's yet again, we ran into a Salamander I would have wielded the Lava Whip on myself if I could have.

Fay had been Loam's on again, off again girlfriend. When we'd gone to the Deep she'd taken up with his cousin.

I shifted to my leopard form, and stepped between Fay and the Terraling.

"I'm watching over her, Fay. Leave the Dirt Girl to me."

Fay let out a low laugh. "Oh, then she'll be dead within

the week. Well done, bad luck cat." She patted my head—harder than she had to—and strolled away, still laughing. That people would think I had deliberately let my charges die... it was the insult of all insults.

Dirt girl reached over and ran her fingers over my head.

"Don't listen to them."

The growl that slipped out of me was out of my control. "We are not friends, Dirt Girl. Not by a long shot. I do this because I must." I shifted back to my housecat form and stalked away, my emotions ranging from the need to be beside her, and the desire to be away from her. To be free of watching over anyone.

Yet I knew that at some point I would have to come to terms with what my life was. One way or another.

4

Dirt Girl and Cactus headed for the Pit, and of course I went with them.

At the Pit though, things shifted yet again.

"Lark, do not walk to the edge. Go to your belly. If you get a waft of fumes, you could pass out and fall in," I said, a shot of worry slipping through me.

She did as I told her, going to her belly. I clung to her back, staying with her. Where she went, I went.

Hanging onto the edge, she peered into the pit.

"Hypnotizing."

"No swimming," I muttered softly into her ear.

Without any warning, she wriggled about, forcing Cactus to grab her ankles. Fear laced each breath I took as I dug my claws in deep to her leather vest so I wouldn't fall. What was she thinking? Had she lost her mind?

None of my other charges had been this reckless . . . no that wasn't entirely true. The first had been like this.

Yes, Talan had been exactly like this, reckless and bold to a fault. It was why I'd lost him.

I stared at the Terraling's hands as she gripped the rock.

The stone molded under her fingers, making perfect handholds.

From what I knew of Terralings that was an old ability. One that had been lost long before my time even.

"We need to discuss this later. You shouldn't be able to mold rock like that," I said.

Using her handholds she flipped over the edge and dropped in a crouch to the floor below the ledge.

The smell of firewyrms overwhelmed me. Dirt Girl leaned forward, cooing softly to two hatchlings. Like tiny, sinuous white dragons, they stared at us, hissing. I could understand them, but the shocking part was, so could she.

How in the name of the mother goddess was that possible?

A thump behind us snapped my head around.

Mouse turds.

Coal, the Ender she thought was a traitor stood behind us. So much for keeping them apart. "Get back, idiot, you don't know what they are capable of."

He grabbed Dirt Girl's arm and jerked her hard enough to send us tumbling ass over teakettle, right out into open space. I let out a screech as I dug my claws deeper into the leather.

No matter what, I wasn't letting her go. Even if it meant I would fall to my death with her.

A flash of white scales and our momentum was stopped and we were being held above the ground.

The male firewyrm had us and scrambled us back up to the ledge.

What we saw when we peered over was the young female firewyrm lying on the ground, blood pooling around her and staining her white scales; Coal stood over her with his black club raised.

"Get away from her," the Terraling snapped as she scrambled forward. She called the earth and it threw Coal backward into the wall, smacking his head hard enough to knock him out.

She ran to the firewyrm, laying her hands on her side.

"Spirit can heal, Dirt Girl. I don't know how, but I know it can. If it isn't too late," I said softly. I was sure she wouldn't try. To use Spirit was to lose a piece of yourself every time you did so. For her to try on a creature of no consequence, someone she didn't even know, was beyond unlikely.

Dirt Girl closed her eyes and Spirit flickered through her, pumping into the lifeless body. She would try and save her?

Now do you see the value in Larkspur?

I did see it, and it still scared me. More than if she were like the others. Because if she was this strong of heart and soul, this sound of mind and morals . . . how much worse would it be when I lost her?

The answer is simple, my cat. Don't lose her.

Don't lose her.

I licked Lark's cheek, swiping away tears she didn't seem to know were there. "You can't save her, Dirt Girl. She's gone too long. That is why Spirit fights you, I believe. I think she was already beyond your reach."

Saying goodbye to Scar, as she so aptly named him, she climbed up onto the ledge to find Cactus out cold with a goose egg on his head. Without hesitation, she healed him, though I felt the dip in her energy.

Our bigger problem was Fiametta showing up.

The queen surprised me, but more so because Jag, her familiar was behind her. His eyes met mine and he slowly shook his head. There was nothing he could do to stay her hand.

I'd already known that.

Coal pulled himself up behind us.

I knew what was coming, there was no way around it. Coal would fight us on this, would try to make it look like Lark was a troublemaker. I whispered into her ear, "He will not go down easy. Be wary."

Coal walked right into the trap we'd set, laying claim to hurting Cactus which only pissed off Fiametta, if the tightening around her eyes was any indication. I may have never been her familiar, but I'd known her since she was a child and she'd always had a wicked temper. Even if she was better at controlling it now.

I was proud of the way Lark handled the back and forth between herself, the queen, and Coal. Setting out the way he'd fooled the queen and gotten into her bed.

Lark turned and started to walk away.

"Stop," Fiametta said.

We turned to see Coal sprinting away.

Cactus pulled down the archway Coal was headed for effectively blocking him. The Ender spun and pointed his club at Fiametta.

The queen would deal with him, and we would be free to go.

At least, that was what I thought.

Lark pulled me from her shoulder and threw me *behind* her as she leapt in front of Fiametta.

Putting herself in danger while trying to protect me.

Heart beating wildly, I knew it was a good move politically. But I didn't think that was why the Terraling had done it.

She'd done it because it was the right thing to do.

She *was* going to be the death of me.

While they fought, Lark used Spirit on Coal. I could feel

it flow out of her and into him in a thin trickle, loosening his tongue.

"The first night you bedded the queen, you were searching for something in her room. What was it?" she asked.

Beside me the queen went stock-still and I knew Lark was in trouble. It was a split-second decision I made. Shifting into my leopard form, I leapt forward, knocking her to the ground as Fiametta unleashed a wave of lava over our heads. I felt the heat through my thick fur.

I stared at where Coal had been, now nothing but a pile of ash and a few bits of charred bone.

Lark buried a hand into the thick fur around my neck. "Thanks."

"That's four times now, Terraling," I said.

Her throat bobbed as she swallowed hard. "I think you'll get at least a few more chances to pull my ass from the fire before we're out of here."

"I believe you may be right."

5
―――

Of course, one fight in a day wasn't enough for my charge.

We'd barely gotten back to Brand's home when Maggie jumped Lark. The two women rolled around, and it wasn't until Maggie started to drag Dirt Girl toward the lava flow that I started to worry.

I shouldn't have though. I needed to remember what I already knew about my Terraling.

She was a survivor.

With a quick jerk of her legs, she had Maggie on the ground and was repeatedly slamming the Salamander's head into the hard stone.

Smoke and Cactus rebuked her as she stood, breathing hard from the exertion and adrenaline from the fight.

I meowed at her and she held out her arms. I leapt up and worked my way up to her shoulder. "You should have smashed her at least twice more," I said.

She looked up at me, her eyes wide with shock. "You aren't going to tell me I should have let her pulverize me?"

I snorted and shook my head. "No, showing weakness in

the Pit will get you killed. The others fear you now; they saw you beat Maggie's ass in a matter of seconds. That is why she came at you. You've beaten her once and she lost standing, losing to a mere dirt girl. Now you've beaten her a second time. She will look for another way to get at you. So we will have to be extra vigilant."

Which was true, we'd have to watch out for Maggie. But for far longer than Lark probably realized. Maggie would wait now, wait for a moment when Lark was at her weakest before she struck. It could be years from now, but Salamanders had a long memory when it came to those they thought had wronged them.

Once more inside Brand and Smoke's home, the family sat for dinner. Already word had spread of Lark's fight with Maggie.

Lark tried to brush it off as nothing. That would not do at all. She deserved props for beating a superior fighter.

I stretched, my back arching as I stepped off Lark's lap and onto the table. I would do my charge the honor she deserved. "Terralings are not to brag. They're humble, unlike you lizards."

Brand seemed to be holding back a smile as I crossed the table. Smoke glowered but only for a second.

I pushed onto my back legs, front paws stretched into the air. "Magma leapt at her from behind, and Dirt Girl sensed it coming. She rolled with Magma tackling her. And *BAM!* the first punch smashed its target." I dropped to all fours and rolled over then popped into the air to land flat on my belly. I loved telling stories, but I would not admit that to anyone.

"What happened next?" Brand's youngest son whispered, his tiny fists pressed under his chin.

I dragged myself across the table with my front claws,

weaving one way and then the other as though stalking prey. "Magma raced backward, dragging the Terraling by her ankles. Right to the lava flow."

Tinder gasped and his fists shook with suppressed emotion. "What then?"

Slithering on my belly until I was hidden behind one of the dishes, I paused. "It looked as though Magma would throw her into the lava flow. But the Terraling used her legs, jerking Magma off balance, cracking their heads against one another."

"And because she is a Terraling, her skull is harder than Magma's?" Tinder asked and I rolled onto my back and jabbed my four feet into the air as if in a four-legged boxing match.

"Exactly." I paused again, and then rolled into attack position, unable to keep my body from wiggling with suppressed adrenaline. "Dirt Girl grabbed Magma by the shoulders and slammed her against the ground three times." I bobbed my head up and down. "*BAM BAM BAM*. Each time harder than the previous until she was satisfied Magma would not be coming around anytime soon." With the last word I leapt toward Tinder, landing right in front of his face. He squealed and laughed and I sat, looking over my shoulder at Lark.

She smiled at me, and in that smile I saw the possibility in her . . . maybe she was the one I'd been waiting for all these years. Damn her for being a Terraling.

After dinner, we retired to the room Lark had been given. She lay, her breathing anything but slow. I had a bad feeling about this.

The boom of the night bells swelled over us. We should have fallen asleep within seconds.

"Damn, you truly are a child of Spirit, aren't you?" I whispered.

"How do you know this? How do you know anything about Spirit?"

I debated how much to tell her, how much of my past she deserved to know. I told her about my first charge, about how he'd had me from the time I was very small. How he'd wielded Spirit.

She scooped me up and pressed her face against me. With her eyes closed, shut tight like a child afraid of what the night held, she clung to me and I purred. This was where I belonged.

"I'm so glad you are here," she whispered. "No matter what happens."

I licked her cheek. "So am I, Dirt Girl. But if you tell anyone, I will claw your face to ribbons while you sleep."

Laughing softly, she set me down.

It didn't take long for us to find our way into trouble yet again though. The healer's rooms did not hold much information that I could sniff out. Yet Lark seemed determined to find something to prove her and her compatriot's innocence.

Nosing the different salves and jars, I searched through everything I could.

"Why do so many Salamanders get burned when they are immune to the flames?" she asked.

"Normally they don't but lately there have been injuries of that kind for many of them. Usually the salves are saved for those who are visiting the Pit," I jumped onto a second counter that ran around the entire room. The jar of nepeta, my namesake, made me sneeze. "Occasionally a death occurs because a child who is too young tries to swim in the lava."

Lark shuddered, and her eyes filled with pain. "Why would they let them do that?"

"They don't. These are children in their early teenage years who believe they are invincible. One of my charges was just such a child."

Ahh, my little red headed darling. She would have been a mighty Salamander if she'd been able to keep her temper in check. A dare. She'd jumped into the deep end on a dare from a boy she'd had a crush on.

And I'd been too far away to prevent her from doing it. Only by a few inches, but it was enough that she'd succumbed to the lava before I could reach her. Screaming for me as she sank down.

Peta. Save me.

Breaking my heart for the third time. Breaking my soul for the first.

"Peta—"

The sound of feet clicking on the stone snapped my head around and pulled me out of my memories. "Shhhh." I hissed, twitching my ears. "Hide. Someone is coming."

Lark slid under one of the beds and I crouched in a shadow on the floor against the counter.

The doors opened and in swept a dark cloaked figure. There was no scent to the person, no hint as to whether it was a man or a woman.

The dark cloaked one searched the room and then paused. "Who is here? I can sense you."

This person started toward the bed Lark was crouched under. I let out a meow, pitching it high and loud as I leapt onto the counter. Trotting along the length of it, I made sure my asshole was pointed right at the dark cloaked one.

"Damn cats. I hate felines. The first thing I'll do when I rule the Pit as queen is kill all you snotty creatures."

Female. And not a nice one by the sound of it.

She left and Lark crept out.

We found the papers that listed the Enders Lark had injured and their wounds. How they were fine but then found dead on the morning check by the healers. This proved her and the other Terraling weren't guilty of killing those Enders. Hurrying, we headed back the way we'd come. The torch went out but we were close enough that I could lead her.

"This way," I called to her.

"This way, Larkspur."

The voice was not one I recognized.

"Dirt girl!" I yelled.

"This way, Lark," the voice said again.

She didn't answer. I flicked an ear back and the sound of feet shuffling told me she was close, despite the other voice. Keeping my pace up, I took the turns, calling back to her at various points.

The other voice faded and then so did the sounds of footsteps.

Breaking out of the tunnels, I turned.

Lark was not behind me.

Heart thumping, I stared into the dark tunnel. "Dirt Girl, that is not funny. Come out."

Nothing.

I reached for the bond between us.

Nothing.

Panic set in. How could I have lost her? She was right behind me?

Diving into the tunnels again was stupid. I might be able to scent her but I was no wolf with the ability to track. Meowing softly to myself, I paced back and forth in front of the opening.

A torchlight behind me spun me around. The prick was headed my way.

"What are you doing?" I snapped at him, my fear for Lark making me prickly.

"I woke up. I think Lark did it. She used to call me like this when we were kids."

Spirit. She was alive and using Spirit to bring Cactus to her. But why not me?

The answer was simple, she was not sure she could trust me yet. And I couldn't blame her.

"Can you find her?"

"I think so, but she'd deep in the tunnels."

He led the way, but I walked right beside him. There was no way I was going to tell him I couldn't feel the bond between Lark and me. "Do you really love her, or are you playing with her heart?"

"Playing matchmaker now?"

"No. I'm her protector."

"I've loved her since we were children, Peta. I would do anything for her."

"Even give her up when she loves another?" I was guessing, but whenever she thought of her fellow Ender, her heart and soul beat a little louder. Not that I was telling Cactus her feelings for the other Terraling was not that different from the way she felt when he was around.

The sounds of voices echoed through the tunnel and Cactus smartly put the torchlight out. We ducked into a side tunnel as Fiametta and two guards passed by.

"I don't care if it is the middle of the night, I think she has something to do with this," the queen snapped.

There was only one *she* that would have the queen up and moving at this hour.

Lark.

As soon as they passed, I bit Cactus on the leg. "Hurry, prick."

He lit the torch and we were off once more, taking turns and corners as fast as we could.

When we rounded the last corner and Lark was ahead of us, I couldn't help myself. With a burst of speed I bolted toward her, leaping up and into her arms. We had to hurry, but I needed to feel that she was okay.

Clinging to Lark, I questioned her. "Dirt Girl, who was that calling to you?"

She looked at me, then then back to Cactus. "You heard him too?"

"Yes." I dug my claws deeper into her clothes, the tips brushing along her skin. She wasn't going to disappear on me again. "I tried to stop you but you couldn't hear me and then . . . I couldn't find you." I couldn't help the full body shiver that ran through me.

"I don't know who he is, but he can manipulate Spirit; he made it sound like you were calling to me," she said.

A low rumbling hiss escaped. "But you stopped him?"

"For now. He took the papers."

Of course he did. The only proof we had that Lark and her fellow Ender were innocent. "He will be back, you think? We will get the papers from him then."

I had to believe it. But for now, we had to get Lark back to Brand's home without Fiametta knowing that she'd ever left.

The prick had a hidden tunnel all picked out and we scurried through it. Past the houses with only a little difficulty, we were back in Brand's home only moments before the queen.

"Just hurry!"

She flopped into the bed and pulled the sheets up

seconds before the queen banged the door open and began her accusations of Lark's whereabouts.

I leapt to the floor, stretching. "My queen, Dirt Girl has been here all night and I have slept beside her. What you are suggesting would imply that she has some sort of strength against our magic."

Fiametta's eyes flicked between me and the Terraling. She bent and scooped me up, shocking me. Mouse turds, I knew what was coming.

She held me up to her face. "And why should I believe you, bad luck cat?"

"Because my heart is here in the Pit, no matter where I am assigned by the mother goddess." I tried to imbue my words with as much sincerity as I could.

The queen's hands began to put pressure on me, her eyes never leaving mine as my ribs cracked under the strength of her fingers. Heat flowed from there through my muscles, breaking apart tendons and tearing at my ligaments. This was a trick I knew all too well.

Once before she had questioned me like this.

I'd broken under her hands, the pain had been so unexpected. But not this time.

She lowered me to the floor, then left the room. I could barely breathe past the injuries.

"Pick me up, Dirt Girl."

She bent and did as I asked. I curled onto her shoulder with a sigh.

Her feet stopped in the threshold of the room. "Peta, did she hurt you?"

"It is her way with familiars, to get them to be honest." My breathing was ragged and I knew several of my ribs were out of place. I expected her sympathy. But not what came next.

Rage flashed through her; anger on my behalf. She strode out the door and through the house.

Fiametta stood waiting with her arms crossed but Lark didn't slow. She all but slammed their faces together, using her body to push the queen back. "If you touch my familiar again—ever—I will pull this mountain down on your head. Do you understand?"

I let out a whimper. Not fear, but disbelief. She was not only standing up for me, but standing up for me against Fiametta. The person who held more power over her than anyone else. The person who held her friend's life in the balance.

I told you she was worth it.

Stop gloating, you were right was all I could manage in my thoughts. The mother goddess was right. Larkspur was worth every bit of pain.

We followed the queen to the throne room, and Lark was able to see her friend Ash. Perhaps more than a friend by they way she kissed him and the rush of emotions I felt along the bond between us; she loved him.

Ash was taken back to the dungeon and Fiametta left us in the throne room, alone.

The haze of hurt kept me from being at my finest, and it wasn't until Lark began to question me over the library that I managed to truly pull myself up out of the fog.

"The rules here are strict, Peta. And everyone follows them to the letter. Is there a place, like a library where I can look for maybe a loophole? Some way we can get Ash out?"

"No libraries here." I shook my head in an over exaggerated way despite the pain rippling from the movement. I needed her to understand I wasn't telling the truth without saying I wasn't telling the truth.

Simplicity at its best.

I blinked slowly several times, willing her to understand that the worst place to discuss things was right there, right where the queen's throne sat. "I think we should go see your friend Cactus. He has some plants I'd like to taste."

Thank the mother goddess, she seemed to get the message.

And we were off to find the prick yet again.

6

Back at Cactus's home, things didn't go quite as I planned. As he tried to convince Lark he hadn't slept with Maggie, all I could think was that he was protesting an awful lot for his supposed innocence.

"You do whatever you want, prick," I snapped, wanting nothing more than to use his groin for a scratching post, "I need to speak with my charge alone."

Cactus laughed softly. "Maybe you will make her a good familiar, bad luck cat. At least you're loyal."

I didn't even try to stop the low hiss that slipped past my lips, or the way my fur stood at attention. He was mocking me, and hurting Lark. A very bad combination as far as I was concerned. Lark bent and scooped me up, and I had to fight the wave of nausea that rolled over me. My body hurt from the tip of my nose to the tip of my tail, but I didn't want Lark to put me down. Being close to her helped soothe the pain.

"A room, Cactus," she said softly.

He gestured to the left and a doorway opened. "Lark, you know me. Maggie isn't my type in the least."

She nodded, and through the bond, I felt her certainty about his motives solidify. She trusted him. I wouldn't have given in to him so easily. "I know, Cactus," she said, "Still, it looked bad." Lark stopped in the doorway, and placed a hand on his chest when he would follow us. And yet again she surprised me by looking to me for advice. "Peta, this is your call."

I didn't want to trust him. I knew too much about him and his past, about the way he'd played women for fools. Yet she seemed determined to see him in a different light. A sigh slipped out of me. "If you trust him, then I will too. He may hear what I have to say."

Once in the room, I knew that I had to give myself over to this once and for all. I would be Larkspur's familiar through and through. I told her the secret about Loam, about the place of knowledge and how it could help them maybe save her friend.

But it wasn't a place to take lightly. I shivered thinking of the way Loam had drawn my energy from me in order to open the doors, the hurt he'd carelessly inflicted on me so he could avoid taking responsibility for his actions.

"Peta, take us there."

"Now?" She had to be kidding. It was late, the night bells would toll soon and if we were caught . . . this time I knew there would be no turning back for the queen. She would kill us both.

Lark nodded, her eyes never leaving mine. "Yes. Now."

Like that, we were off.

As we walked, she held me gently in her arms, but even so, my breathing was rough. I tried to keep it even, so she wouldn't feel it. But there was no denying the gurgle in my lungs, or the way my body had a continuous tremor running through it. Maybe she wouldn't notice. An unspoken question hovered around us, so I answered it.

"That's why I can't shift right now," I said. "A shift when I'm so injured would surely puncture my air bags and I would be of no use."

Her one hand stroked along my back, gently, as soft as feathers being brushed against my fur. I closed my eyes and sank deeper into her arms. Time and patience was what I needed to heal this kind of injury. Neither of which we truly had. If a fight came, I would be all but useless to Lark.

"Cactus, stop a minute," she said, then directed her words to me. "We're connected, aren't we?"

I narrowed my eyes, wondering what she was getting at. "We are."

"And I can draw energy from you, if I need to be healed?"

"Yes." That was something she already understood, so why the question now?

She closed her eyes. "Then let's reverse the flow."

"No, it doesn't work that way. It's not how things are supposed to be," I said, already knowing that her idea, though generous, was silly. Familiars did not draw from their charges, it wasn't possible.

And yet I felt Spirit weave through me and with it the smell of cedar and lush greens—not unlike the haven Cactus had created. The smells preceded the shifting of bones and flesh as my body healed itself within seconds. But it wasn't only the power of Spirit that had healed me, Lark had pushed some of her own life force into me as well, giving me some of herself. I gasped while Lark swayed lightly under me.

"Stupid, Dirt Girl! You aren't supposed to sacrifice your life for me. It's supposed to be the other way around!" I glared up at her while I fought the tears that prickled. No one had ever done anything like that before. Not even my first charge and he would have been the only one who could have.

Lark shrugged and I leapt from her arms, immediately shifting to my snow leopard form.

I didn't know how to feel. Terralings were supposed to be useless and stupid. The lowest of all the elementals in power and worth. Yet she was showing me minute to minute, she was neither of those. Her heart was stronger than all twelve of the charges I'd held onto in the past.

"I can't have you slowing us down," she said.

My back stiffened. "I would not have slowed you down."

The prick patted me on the base of the tail. "Yeah, you were, kitten."

If he had not been there to help us, I would have spun and raked him in the face with my claws. But that would have slowed us down and likely Lark would have wasted precious energy healing him.

Going ahead of them, I led they way while they spoke. What in the name of the mother goddess was I supposed to feel now?

Stop fighting this, Nepeta. You are meant to be with Larkspur. I have trained you by sending you with each of the other charges. From each of them you have learned and grown. I needed a familiar who is strong and smart and loyal to the core for my chosen one. That familiar is you. Do not doubt it for one second.

The mother goddess spoke to me softly, but with a strong flavor of rebuke in her words. She was right, I'd been fighting this even while a part of me had wanted to let Lark in.

I warred with myself, vacillating between bonding truly with the Terraling, and keeping her at tail's length.

We reached the tiger fountain and I explained to Lark how it worked. Or at least, how I thought it worked with there being some sort of latch or button within the boiling water.

Lark of course put her hand in, and found the latch on the first try. But even that quick dunk into the boiling water hurt her. Her arm was bright red and in spots pale blisters were starting to appear, though I didn't think she could see them yet with her eyes.

"Draw on me, Dirt Girl. Loam did. I know the pain will be temporary," I said.

She nodded and the pain flowed from her into me. The pain was not new; I'd bore it many times while serving as a guide and familiar to Loam. Under my fur, my skin prickled. At least I was able to spread the hurt over my entire body rather than have it concentrated on one section. My skin heated until it felt as though I had been in the sun for days with my bare skin exposed and then my fur stitched back on. Not as bad as being dunked in boiling water, but not exactly pleasant either.

Lark stopped drawing on me though too soon; her arm was still several shades too pink and would be noticed. That was something we did not need.

I pushed up against her. "Fiametta will know. You should take more from me."

"I'll wear a long-sleeve shirt," she said. "I can't take all your strength, Peta. I need you. And I don't like causing you pain. How often did Loam come here?"

"Daily." The word slipped out of me before I thought better of it and it was only then that I allowed myself to recall why I didn't want to bring Lark here. What if she wanted to come back again, and again, and again? While I'd been in the Pit with Loam, my body had never truly healed.

Always I was trying to heal, only to have to take on his burns again.

Lark looked at me, and compassion flowed through the bond. She didn't have to say the words for me to know what she was thinking.

She would not do that to me.

We went inside the tiny space of a library, searching for a way to free her friend. And to get us all out of the Pit in one piece. The time ticked by far faster than I'd hoped and the night bells tolled without warning. There was no denying them this time as fatigue knocked all three of us to the floor. I curled up beside Lark and let out a heavy sigh of relief.

The dream that sucked me under was one I had not had for many years. A dream of the past, of my first charge.

Talan grinned at me, a wide smile under a pair of sparkling blue eyes. His hair hung to his shoulder and was messy and wild. "Nepeta, I've missed you."

I ran to him, leaping into his arms and burying my nose into the crook of his neck. "Talan, oh, you have no idea how I've missed you."

His hands stroked over my back, ruffling my fur. "Cat, you've got a challenge ahead of you with this one. You know that, right?"

"I do. She is not you, Tal. You will always be my favorite."

He laughed, and then held me out from him. "That is not true. I see the bond between you two already and it is strong after a single day. She is the heart mate you have been waiting for. But that makes me happy."

A soft cry escaped me. "No."

"Yes, she is good for you. A little bit wild, a little bit reckless, but also grounded. The perfect blend of Spirit and Earth." He put me on the ground and beckoned to me. "Come, walk with me a moment."

I trotted beside him, feeling like I was two hundred years younger and that perhaps all my lost charges had been nightmares that I'd finally woken up from.

"No, this is the dream, Nepeta," he said and there was more than a bit of sadness. "I'm sorry I had to let you go. It was as the mother goddess wanted."

Let me go . . .surely he didn't think it was his fault that the Sylph had killed him, did he? "What do you mean let me go? I saw you get sucked up in the tornado, I felt our bond break as death took you. There was nothing you could have done to stop that."

He glanced at me and gave me a smile. "Peta. I broke the bond between us. The mother goddess had other plans for you."

My feet stopped as if grabbed by a bog of death mud. "What?"

"I am not dead, Peta."

I leapt for him, not sure if I wanted to wrap my paws around his neck or claw his eyes out. I clung to him and he held me as I screamed in his ear. "You bastard, do you know what I've been through? Do you know the things I've suffered and the reality of my life? Do you not think for one second I was . . .you thought I wasn't good enough for you any longer." The words slipped out of me and I pushed away, running into the fog of my dream.

He was like all the others. I wasn't good enough and so he'd let me go. No, the mother goddess thought I wasn't good enough for him and she'd made him let me go.

That bitch.

"Nepeta." Talan was suddenly in front of me and I skidded to a stop. Damn dreams and their lack of reality. "I am alive, and it is almost time for you to bring Larkspur to me. I will train her."

"She doesn't need you," I spit out, as I arched my back. "She's stronger than you."

His lips twitched. "You see, already you have chosen her over me."

I had, and I didn't care. "She would never put me aside. Not even for the mother goddess."

Talan crouched in front of me. "Perhaps that is true. Will you bring her to me, when I come to you again?"

I hunched my shoulders. "I will give her the choice. I will not force her."

"That is all I ask."

Hunching myself further, I fought the tears and then gave up, looking to him. "You broke my heart, Tal. You broke it into a thousand tiny pieces and I have been trying to fix it for so long. And then Lark comes into my life and those pieces are flowing back together. Having you show up now . . . it isn't fair."

"No, but that is how the mother goddess works, isn't it? Fair is not her middle name, kitten."

I had to smile at that, and it was as if my smile broke the dream apart.

Lark was already awake, but her thoughts were being kept from me. I wasn't worried, but I should have been. Talan was right about her, she was a bit wild, and also grounded. A deadly combination when it came to her setting her mind on something.

7

As we left the hidden library, Lark gave Cactus directions. So she *did* have a plan. My curiosity got the better of me.

"What are you doing, Dirt Girl?"

"I'm going to confess," she said as if it were the most natural thing in the world to take someone else's place in death. Like she was telling me we were going to have tea and cookies with a friend.

"No!" I roared, leaping in front of her and physically blocking her from moving forward. "I will not allow it. You and I both know those Enders were killed after they were healing. You would at most have a lashing, and yet even that would kill you here in the Pit! Your death is not deserved, Larkspur. You can't do this." I couldn't stop my voice from shaking. I could not lose her. Damn Talan for putting the thought in me. I did not want it to be true.

I would not admit even to myself that she was quickly becoming my world. She dropped to her knees and wrapped her arms around my neck. I pressed my mouth against her collarbone, my teeth chattering against her skin.

I could not keep my emotions in check—especially after seeing Talan alive and realizing how much Lark already meant to me. I had to stop her from this madness.

No matter what it took, no matter what I had to do I had to keep her from confessing.

"Peta, I don't plan to die," she said. "Belladonna will get me out of this and if I have to . . . I will fight my way out."

I gasped and then pulled back to stare at her. A little wild? Perhaps more than a bit. None of my other charges had ever even considered fighting another elemental, even when it was warranted.

"I'm not like the other elementals. I won't go down without a fight. Trust me. Please." She begged me both with her words and the bond between us to understand her. And a part of me did. But the other part . . .

"You would be banished, anathema to all who met you. Your life would be over; you would be the walking dead. For what? A single life freely given in exchange for yours?" Could she truly mean to do this?

"No one will die, Peta."

That was easy for her to say. She was young and hadn't seen how very hard the world could be, and how cruel the mother goddess was at times.

She put a hand on my head, her fingers working deep into my fur. "Peta."

I dropped my head and rolled my eyes up so I could look at her still. "Larkspur, please do not ask me to do this. To watch you offer up your life. You will be the thirteenth charge the mother goddess has given me. I cannot bear to watch you die, too."

"Walk with me." She put her hip against my shoulder and I reluctantly let her push me so we were again moving forward. I knew she could find her way to the throne room.

There was the large statue of Fiametta already twinkling at us from a distance. In only a few more strides we were at the large doors. Fiametta's voice could be heard clearly, at least to my ears.

"Trust me to come out of this alive, Peta," Lark said.

"That is what my first Spirit charge said right before he died trying to save a friend," I whispered. Talan had done that very thing, told me to trust him as he dove into the tornado to save his friend. And they'd both died. Or at least, I thought they had.

Lark faced Fiametta like only a true warrior could. Without fear for herself, only thinking of those she wanted to save.

It took all my strength not to leap in front of her and knock Fiametta flat, to urge Lark to run and escape the Pit. To make her see that there was no good way this could end.

Trust. The word was hard for me to swallow, yet I did anyway. Lark had a plan, and I would trust in it as she had trusted in me to give her good advice. A relationship of give and take, of trust and understanding.

Even Talan hadn't trusted me completely, for if he had there would have been no deception at the end. He would have broken the bond between us and walked away. I'm not sure that it would have been any easier, but it would have at least been honest.

Fiametta led Lark to her personal chamber, and when I moved to follow, the queen stopped me, her blue-eyed glared hot on my fur. "This is not for you, familiar. I see your hand in this; you took her to the library, giving her access that only Loam had." She pointed at the paper Lark still clutched.

I tipped my head to one side, a burning desire to lash

out growing strong in me. "You are not my queen any longer, Fiametta. I obey Larkspur, no one else."

Fiametta's hands clutched at her side, and her eyes. Oh, if looks could kill I'd be dead and buried ten feet under.

Lark put a hand on my head and calm flowed through her into me. "Wait for me. Please."

Reluctantly, I nodded and sat outside the door. "I will come if you call."

The door slammed behind them and I sat quietly, breathing slowly in through my nose and out my mouth. Focusing on the rise and fall of my chest and trying not to think of all the awful things the queen could be doing to Larkspur. This was the part of being a familiar that I hated. The moments where I could do nothing to help.

Yet the bond between Lark and me was steady and her life force was strong giving me a measure of certainty that it would be all right. A sudden burst of power flowed through her, disrupting my meditation. Earth, that was what she'd pulled on. Only a second, and then the power was gone and the ground was still.

"Peta."

Lark called for me and I spun, pushing the doors open. Fiametta was sunk to her neck in the rock. I lowered myself to my belly and crept forward.

"Lark, what has happened?"

"I need you to get Cactus. Hurry," she said, and a thread of worry floated between us.

Without a word, I turned and bounded away. Finding Cactus was easier said than done.

I all but slammed into Brand as I rounded the first corner.

"Bad luck cat, what are you doing here? Where is Lark?"

"I need to find Cactus," I spit out, ignoring the jab at me. Now was not the time.

"I saw him headed this way." He turned and pointed and I was off and running. Why Lark needed Cactus, I didn't know but I had to get him fast. The queen would have something up her sleeve, that much I knew. Fiametta hadn't risen to power because of bloodlines or good looks. No, she'd taken the throne with sheer strength and intelligence.

Three corners and I picked up the scent of Cactus—a little bit fire and a little bit dirt. "Cactus!" I yelled his name and he sprinted toward me, he green eyes meeting mine.

"Is she okay?"

"Yes, but she needs your help right now. You must hurry!" I snapped, swinging a paw at him with my claws outstretched to get the point across.

Brand was right behind me when I turned. "Out of my way, Ender."

"If Lark is in trouble, I can help," he said.

"Fine, but don't dilly dally."

Of course, it was the wrong choice to bring the Ender, but I never thought he would turn on Lark.

I was so very wrong.

As the crossbow slammed into her shoulder she stumbled backward, reaching for her spear but I knew what was coming, could see it on Fiametta's face. I leapt in front of Lark as a ring of fire burst up around us, like a cage that increasingly shrank.

Fiametta stood over us. "These two men are loyal to me, you didn't really think any negotiation we made in front of them would hold, did you?"

Pinned to the ground, I laid my body over Lark's, protecting her from the heat. It was all I could do. We were sunk, Fiametta would kill us both. Yet I knew that if I had to die, I was glad it was with Lark.

She stared up at Fiametta. "You know, I'm beginning to think the rulers of all the families are assholes."

Another time I would have laughed because she was right. All the rulers *were* assholes.

We were dragged off to the dungeon and I was chained to the wall by my neck. I couldn't help but pace the small length I was given. This was not the first time I'd been chained up, but I didn't take it lightly that the last time had been while I was Talan's familiar. Something about the Spirit users obviously got them into trouble.

Lark's friend, or supposed friend, lashed out at her.

"We aren't going to survive this. I thought I could at least get you out of here and now you've gone and screwed that up."

"What?" she whispered. "Are you serious?"

"One thing, I asked one thing of you—to go with Brand and save your own life—and you couldn't even do that."

Her pain cut through me, not of the physical variety but through her heart. This man who hurt her, she loved him. I could feel those ties as surely as I could feel my own ties to her. And he was cruel to her. A cry slipped out of me as I strained against the chains in an attempt to reach her. To comfort her.

Ash softened his voice. "I was only trying to make you angry, so you could reach your power."

What an idiot. Men and their brilliant ideas. I wanted to snap at him that it would have been better if he'd hit her if he'd wanted to piss her off.

Belladonna though saved him from my tongue lashing as she swept in and had Lark and me unchained and brought before Fiametta once more.

This time, Belladonna took the stage and brought everyone to a standstill with her reasoning: Lark could not be held accountable for the deaths of the Enders because she herself was not yet an Ender.

A sigh of relief slipped out of me, but it did not last. I should have known.

Fiametta had Lark read the second part of the papers, about the punishment at the choice of the ruler offended.

Fiametta pointed the coiled leather at Lark. "Strip her."

Belladonna gasped. "You can't truly mean to do to this."

"Cassava has obviously misled you, little Terraling. We are not friends, and neither are our families." Fiametta uncoiled the leather and her hands lit up as she called on the fire. Like a living snake it wrapped around the leather.

Lark's sister yelled at her, "Lark, fight her!"

No, this was not happening. It couldn't be. To have found Lark only to lose her so swiftly was too unfair to both of us. Fear spread through me like poison. "Lark, this is not a punishment you can survive, the lava whip is deadly to any who don't carry fire in their veins."

"On your knees," Fiametta commanded.

Lark went to her knees, shaking off those who would hold her down.

The lash rose and fell, the sparkling flames along the edge of it so hot they were white. Over and over again it fell. Someone hung onto me, several someones'. Hands were wrapped around my neck, tail, and back legs and it was only then that I realized my teeth were bared as I stared at Fiametta and fought to get to her.

I would rip out the bitch's throat and claw her face to shreds. Larkspur's pain danced at the edge of our bond but she refused to let me help her. Which only left me one choice.

Kill the one who hurt her.

"Enough, you'll kill her!" A voice cut through the madness and the prick—Cactus—stepped between the queen and Lark. Perhaps he did love her after all.

"The punishment is done," Fiametta said while staring hard at Lark. The hands that held me back released me and I ran to my charge.

I pushed my face close to hers, breathing in time with her. "Lark, draw from me."

"No."

Ahh, to have such heart! I knew what she did, she did to spare me. And it made me love her even more. "I will carry her," I said.

Others lifted her onto my back and I slunk into a stalking crouch that allowed me to move forward with very little jarring motion. All the way to Brand's home, I slunk as Lark's wounds seeped into my fur, the blood and fluids leaking her life from her. That she'd survived this far was unbelievable. The only thing I could think was the mother goddess had somehow intervened.

Settling Lark into her room, I shifted back to my housecat form and curled up beside her face, laying my tail over her neck. Purring softly, I sang her the songs of my childhood, those rumbling tunes my mother had caressed my senses with as the wind howled down the mountainside.

The sound of footsteps rolled through to me. Footsteps with a lilt to them. Exactly like I'd heard in the tunnels when Lark had been taken from me.

"Lark, he's coming," I managed to spit out before a darkness overtook me. Not of sleep, but an empty space where I heard and saw nothing and had no idea where I was. Or when I would escape it.

To say I did not like it was an understatement.

I don't know how long I was out, only that when I woke things were much different than before.

Lark was standing and it wasn't that she was up that surprised me. But her back was healed. Or at least, the wounds were closed. Most of the flesh was still missing, leaving gaping holes. I let out a yowl and leapt to the floor. "Lark, your back, it's healed. How can that be? What happened?"

Wobbling as she turned, she shook her head. "The one in the cloak, he did it."

"The one who tried to drop the bridge out from under you? That makes no sense."

She put a hand to her head, confusion rolling over her face. "No, it doesn't."

She lay down, a sigh slipping out of her. "Peta, get Cactus and Ash. Tell them we leave as soon as I wake."

I bolted from the room, but didn't have to go far. The two men were in the kitchen, heads together.

"You two," I snapped and they spun at the same time.

"Is she awake?" they asked in together.

"No, but when she wakes up, we're going," I said before spinning on my haunches and running back to the room. Being apart from her, even that little bit, pulled on my soul. I still did not believe she was truly my heart mate, but she was my charge.

No matter how hard it was, I would look out for her. Even if she was a dirt girl.

8

Of course, when Lark did wake, we did not leave. Her back had been healed by the mother goddess, and now the Terraling sported an imprint of the goddess's touch. A vine of deep green with dark purple thorns wove over her body where the burns had been. I wasn't sure I wanted to know what she'd had to trade for that level of healing.

Though I had a feeling the reason we were not leaving had something to do with it.

It didn't take long for me to see the firestorm I'd been sensing was upon us. The lava flow began to spill out of its confines eating up all those in its path—even the Salamanders.

We had to get out of the Pit; there was no other choice.

Brand gestured to the ladder that would lead us out of the living quarters. "You three get up there. Peta, you can lead them to the Traveling room."

I leapt up several rungs of the ladder before looking back at Lark and Ash. "Hurry."

Unable to hear what Lark said to Brand over the roaring

of the lava lighting up everything in its path, I was not surprised to see that he followed up the ladder. Smart man.

Brand led us toward the Traveling room, stopping at the stairwell that led down to it. We peered past him to stare at the bubbling lava that curled up the steps toward us. That made the decision easy. No going home that way.

He didn't pause though. "The queen has a backup pair of armbands in her chambers. She'll let you use those. I don't know where they will take you though."

"Unless she's using them to get her people out of here," I said, padding ahead of them at a steady trot. There was no point getting fussed at this juncture. We only had to get to the exit and we would be out of the mountain and away from the lava. Easy as far as I was concerned.

Not so easy with Lark.

We found Fiametta in the healer's rooms and we offered to help move the Salamanders out to the main entrance to do exactly what I thought should have been done in the first place.

From the corner of my eye, I saw the queen's familiar, Jag, hanging back. "You told her to do this, didn't you?" I asked.

He nodded. "Yes, but she wouldn't listen. Hours ago, I told her it was time to evacuate, but she refused. Said she could handle it." He snorted softly. "There is no place for familiars in the elemental world anymore, my friend."

I looked from him to Lark, and my heart warmed. "No, we have a place. They only have to remember that we are a part of them."

Lark offered to carry some of the children who'd been burned. I moved beside her. "I can take someone."

Smit snorted. "Bad luck cat, I don't think so."

Lark put a hand on him, tightening her fingers over his

forearm. "Her name is Peta, and if you call her a bad luck cat again, I will forget you are a healer."

His eyes flicked between us. He swallowed hard. And I wanted to shout it from the rooftops. "I thought the rumor was wrong about her being your familiar. Pardon me."

I let out a soft snort and Lark shifted the young girl to my back.

The child leaned forward. "You have a beautiful coat."

Looking back at her, the golden eyes of a fire elemental stared back. So innocent though. "You have beautiful eyes."

She blushed and lay forward, her arms clinging to me.

We left the healer's rooms and headed for the main entrance. The doors led onto a massive field of cherry trees perpetually in blossom, the petals flowing down like a soft, warm snowstorm. At least, if they were open that would be the case. As it was, they were locked down tight and it seemed as though no one was getting out.

Which made things rather touchy when the adult firewyrm showed up.

He burst through a sidewall and advanced on Fiametta. She held up her hand as if that would stop him. He ignored her.

"You think you rule here, but your fear is what rules this place. You are no queen." The lizard snarled and leapt forward with his mouth gaping.

As the firewyrm leapt forward, time slowed. I heard the echo of the mother goddess speak to Lark to save Fiametta.

The Terraling jumped in front of Fiametta and held up both her hands, as she dropped to my knees.

"In the name of the mother goddess, stop!"

Mewling under my breath, I waited knowing that any move I made could be considered aggressive as far as the firewyrm was concerned.

"Who do you think you are that you can stop me with words? Are you like the other one?" the firewyrm growled out.

He lowered his face so he was eye to eye with Lark. My mouth dried up. One bite would cut her in half and there would be nothing I could do to stop him.

She didn't lower her hands. "Fiametta is a bitch, a liar, and a manipulator. She's tried to wipe your people out, punished me with the intention to end my life, and in general being a grade A bitch."

I swung my eyes to look at Fiametta. Her face was closed off, giving away nothing. Surely she would strike Lark down for saying that? Even if it was the truth.

He chuckled. "Yes, all of those things and more. Why do you stop me then from snapping her in half and using her bones to pick my teeth?"

Lark slowly lowered her hands. "Because the mother goddess wants her alive for some unknown reason. And as her chosen one, I will do all I can to make ensure her wishes are fulfilled. If it were my choice, I would let the queen die and another take her position."

He pushed his face forward until they were nose to nose. "You are the one who saved my son and tried to revive my daughter. Spirit walker, your heart is too big for your body."

The firewyrm shook his head at the queen. "Fiametta, only because this one," he tipped his jaw toward Lark, "intervenes and speaks on behalf of the mother goddess will I spare you and your people. But I want my children back."

Lark stood, without a single tremble in her body. "The Salamanders have missing children too. Someone is killing them."

He shook his massive head, the horns that swept over his neck shimmering from side to side. "Sucked into the lava?"

She nodded. "Yes."

"Then they are not dead. It is how our children were taken too. I feel their hearts beating yet. Come to my nest, and perhaps we can find them, Spirit Walker." He backed up, his body disappearing into the hole he'd created.

Of course, just because she'd stopped the firewyrm didn't mean she was a hero. Not to the Salamanders. Around us, the dissent started immediately. Fools and lava suckers.

"How did she stop him?"

"What did they say?"

"Why didn't the queen kill the wyrm?"

Fiametta lifted a hand. "Larkspur. You are the half-breed bastard child that Basileus has kept hidden from the rest of us. Correct? You are Ulani's child."

"Yes," Lark said, without an ounce of regret. Good girl. Stand firm, this was the time to do no less.

"Then we will discuss this once we are outside the mountain. For now I will trust you, not only with my home, but with my families' lives," the queen said.

Fiametta turned and looked at her people. "We will exit through the main entrance, and once outside I will send some of my Enders to deal with the wyrms and the lava."

No one argued with her, not even the Enders. Lark slipped back to where she'd deposited the two kids and bent to scoop them up. They smiled, reaching for her, but she was pushed away.

"Don't touch them, you filthy wyrm lover."

He picked the kids up, their eyes wide as they stared back at her. The Salamanders flowed around Lark as if she were an island in a stream.

I moved up to stand with her. While I'd watched the interaction between Lark and the firewyrm, the little lizard had been taken from my back. "They took her from me too."

Ash waited for us, his arms also empty. "Me, too."

"Guilty by association," Lark murmured.

Those Salamanders who had allowed Lark, Ash, and me to help them rushed away from us as though we had a disease. "Fools, all of them," I muttered low under my breath.

I snorted and shook my body, shrinking to my housecat form. Lark held out her and I leapt up to her.

"You can carry me."

Laughing softly, she placed me on my shoulder. "Thanks, I appreciate the vote of confidence."

Ah, the pain under those words. I wanted to claw the eyes out of those who had struck at her in the past, those who had made her doubt herself.

I sat up straight on her shoulder, looking over everyone's head. The fact we lingered there in the cavern while the lava flows crept closer made my fur tingle. "Why aren't they moving?"

Lark's shoulders rolled underneath me. "Maybe Ash is right and the door is stuck." All around us, the Salamander's heads whipped around to stare at us. Not one seemed pleased to note we still remained there.

Balancing on my back legs, I stood and put my paws on the top of Lark's head for a better view. The doors were indeed closed, not a single speck of daylight coming through. This was not good at all.

"I think that's exactly what has happened. You need to get up there, you two."

They pushed through the crowd with ease; at least that was the upside of being pariahs. Everyone got out of your way.

At the front of the crowd was Maggie, Fiametta, and Cactus who shook his head almost violently.

"I can't reach that side of my powers, my queen. I'm sorry," Cactus said.

Fiametta looked to Lark, her blue eyes shimmering with tears. "And you two, can you open the mountain?"

Ash stepped forward first, laying his hands on the large black door for only a moment before stepping back. "I'm sorry."

Lark was up next. I felt her reach for her powers, felt them slide through her grasp over and over again. The block on her abilities was there as thick and wide as the base of a mountain.

The anger in her spiked and with it the block dissipated. So that truly was the key for her. I had hoped it wasn't the case; anger could only take her so far.

The power within Lark rose to a crescendo pitch and she pushed it toward the door. With a grinding screech the door opened.

Cherry blossoms spilled through the doorway bringing with them their sweet scent and the heady taste of fresh air. But Lark was still sweating, hanging onto her power as if her life depended on it.

"Hurry, get them through!" Lark yelled. Putting my nose in her ear I spoke.

"What's happening?"

The door groaned and creaked, inching closed. "Someone is pushing the doors closed as I'm holding them open."

What Lark couldn't see though was that the Salamanders hadn't moved an inch. They didn't trust her enough to step between the doorway.

"Let it go, Lark," Ash said.

She let go and looked. I was ashamed of the elementals I'd once called my own. A sorrier group of fools I had never known. They wouldn't even take her help to save themselves and their children because of their fear and pride. And I'd thought them the strongest of all the elementals? I had been a fool alongside them.

"What the hell is wrong with you? Why didn't you go through?" she yelled at them; they looked away from her. All except one.

"How can we trust you?" Maggie said, pushing her face right against Lark's. "You could have crumbled the archway on top us as we walked through."

There was more than a murmuring of assent more like a roar of agreement.

"You all just signed your own death warrants," she said softly. Grief flowed from her and into me. Their lives were already lost and she knew it. I closed my eyes thinking of the children who would die because their parents were so unwilling to see that a Terraling *could* help them.

Fiametta motioned for Lark to follow her. "Larkspur, I will beg if I must. I cannot stop the lava flows."

"You could have made them go through the doorway. You could have been the first one through and shown them the way out and this would now *not even be a discussion*," she snapped.

Fiametta's face was carefully blank. "You are right."

For the queen to admit she was wrong? Unheard of. Perhaps the times were changing, though it was too late for her people if she could not drive them to do what they had to do to survive.

Behind us came the cries of the Salamanders and the splashing of lava as it reached the back of the line. People pushed forward, screaming, crying, and begging.

We were jammed against the door along with Fiametta. They would take the doorway now... if Lark could open it.

Mother goddess let her be able to open it.

"Peta, help me," she whispered. "I can't reach the earth unless I'm angry."

"Ash," I called for the two men, "Cactus, get over here."

They pushed through, climbing over people to get to her. Screams echoed up the tunnel as the lava kissed at the heels of those at the back.

Ash and Cactus crouched beside me. "What do you need us to do?"

I curled tighter around Lark's neck. "Show her you trust her. That is the key to breaking through these final bonds she carries."

Cactus didn't hesitate, but wrapped his arms around her from his side, pressing his lips into her hair. "I trust you to save us, Lark. You can do this."

From her right side, Ash placed his hands over hers. "Larkspur, you truly are the best of us, don't doubt it."

She shook as the anger began to build in her once more.

"No," I said. "Let the anger go and hold to the trust and love. That is your way now, Lark. That is the only way."

As the words fell from my lips, the truth of them cut through the wall of denial I'd built around my heart. For the first time since Talan, I let my own anger go. The hurt of being treated like an unwanted guest, of being used and abused by those who should have cared for me the most.

The pain of being seen as the reason those around me died slid from my shoulders, the weight of it, a living thing as it left me. I saw Lark's heart for the first time and realized it truly beat in time with my own.

She *was* my heart mate.

And that knowledge opened a door within me I never

even knew existed. Beyond it was an ability that was legendary amongst familiars...

The time will come when you need this, Nepeta. But not yet, my child. Not yet. Until you gave yourself to her, there would have been no seeing this possibility. Well done.

The mother goddess spoke softly and was gone before I could answer her, or better yet, ask her a question about the ability gifted to me.

The doors in front of us slid open, for both the block on Lark's powers and the block on the exit. The Salamanders rushed forward around us, barely escaping the killing lava flows.

9

The next few moments were some that do not bear repeating. From Blackbird's arrival—and the abomination that he was—to the floor of the cavern dropping out from under us, to the young firewyrm Scar hauling us out of trouble.

The entire time, all I could think about was how much Lark reminded me of Talan, but yet in her own way she was so much more dangerous to her own self. She threw her body in harm's way to save those she loved.

Even to save those she didn't.

As we climbed down the wall that led into the dragonlike firewyrms' domain, Lark's focus shifted. Her eyes traveled over the two men, and her heart rate picked up.

She loved them both. But the distraction of that was poor in its timing. I flicked my tail over her face, drawing her eyes to me for a split second. "Pay attention to the wall you are climbing, not the men."

After that reminder, she was much better, her eyes and mind back on the task at hand.

Scar sat on his haunches, waiting for us at the bottom.

Cactus and Ash dropped in a few seconds later. The young firewyrm gave Cactus a sidelong glance. "You can only take your familiar with you. The others have to wait here."

She put her hands on her hips. "Take her with me where? What are you talking about?"

Scar flicked his head over his shoulder, his tongue darting out and tasting the air. "This tunnel leads to the throne room where the cloaked ones are currently discussing how to wipe us out. They have the children deep in the dungeons."

"Then why doesn't your father get them?" she asked, stepping up beside him. I had to agree with her. The firewyrms were formidable advisories. Why weren't they fighting the cloaked ones?

"Because whenever we get close to them we lose our memory of what we do. That is why we've been attacking the Salamanders. We didn't want to, they were making us." Scar shook his head. "You are the only one who can go in, Spirit Walker. The males must stay here if they are to be safe; they could be forced to hurt you too."

"No, we aren't leaving her." Cactus shook his head.

Ash nodded his agreement though. "Understood."

Cactus stared at him. "You would leave her to do this on her own?"

"She has to." Ash gave Cactus a stony stare. "What if the other Spirit Walker takes control of you, makes *you* fight her? What is she supposed to do then?" He shook his head. "I know all too well how hard it is to fight the compulsion, and the only way to break it is to be touching Lark physically. How do we fight when we can't let go of one another?"

Cactus was still not convinced. "Then how come Peta can go?"

What a fool. "I'm her familiar. I'm protected by Lark's abilities, Prick."

"No more arguing. The longer this takes the more chance we have of those two escaping," Lark said.

As she walked away, I looked back in time to see Ash tackle Cactus to the floor. If I had my pick of the two men, I knew which it would be.

"Lark, don't do this; they'll kill you," Cactus called out.

I swayed on her shoulder, and slowly shook my head. "How little faith he has."

"No, I don't think it's a matter of faith," she said as we followed the shimmering white scales of Scar's back. "I think it's a matter of love."

Of that, I was not so certain. But I wasn't going to argue with her, not then.

Scar led us through a tight tunnel to the throne room. The statue of Fiametta hid the secret exit well. I in all my years had never noticed it. Then again, by the way the edges of the tunnel looked it was perhaps more recent than I had first thought. The dirt was loose and the edges sharp and unworn.

Definitely new.

We approached the throne room doors.

"Peta, get the kids, lead them through the tunnel. Can you do that?" Lark asked, her voice pitched low.

"I can. But then you will go after her alone, won't you?" I already knew the answer but I wanted her to say it. To tell me the truth. "Won't you?"

"Yes, but I've stopped her before, I can do it again. Just hurry. Get those kids out."

I had to trust her. No matter how much I wanted to protect her, I also had to know when to let her lead even if it scared me.

This was one of those moments, and I was terrified I was going to lose her.

In my leopard form, I slunk toward the dungeons, taking a less used entrance. The steam from the rooms rose in great wafting clouds of heat, sinking through my fur to pool against my skin with the high humidity. Keeping my belly to the ground, I worked my way forward carefully, fully expecting there to be a trap waiting.

But there was nothing. And at first I thought perhaps there weren't even any children.

"Peta?"

Tinder . . . that was Tinder's voice.

"Little lizard," I swung my head toward his voice. He was hunched down against the wall farthest from me, a wall of steam between us that spit up in big gusts. His face was twisted. "The steam is too hot, we can't get through."

I approached slowly, my mind racing. Get them out, that was what I was to do. If the steam was burning them, it would burn me too.

But I could heal, and the only way they would be safe would be to get them out. Bunching the muscles in my back legs, I leapt forward, as high as I could and through the top of the steam. The searing heat scorched through my fur as if it were flames and not hot, humid air. I landed lightly, a grimace twisting up my lips. In front of me were close to thirty children.

"Three at a time on my back," I said. Tinder helped the smaller children up first. The littlest one began to cry. "Hang onto her fur. Peta will get us out of here," Tinder said.

His faith in me was enough. I turned carefully, and leapt up and through the steam. Back and forth I went ferrying the children across until they were all out from behind the wall of steam. My belly and legs were scorched clean of fur and my skin oozed with burn pustules.

Breathing hard, I struggled not to limp with the children at my side. Tinder noticed, turned and put a hand on my back. "Peta, you're hurt bad."

"Yes. But I will heal."

Indeed you will. The mother goddess's voice rolled over me and with it the burns on my body receded and fur replaced the pustules. A matter of seconds at most. Tinder nodded as if it were the most natural thing in the world to see the mother goddess's hand at work on a daily basis. "Let's go."

Urging them forward, Tinder and I herded the children out of the dungeon to the tunnel that led to the firewyrms' cavern.

"Tinder, follow this passageway. Cactus and the Terraling man will be waiting for you," I said, pushing them with my nose into the tunnel.

"Where are you going?" His eyes met mine and then his hand brushed along my head. "Aren't you coming with us?"

"Lark needs me," I said. "Be brave, little lizard, and look out for the others."

As soon as the last of them disappeared into the tunnel I spun and ran for the throne room. Pushing the door open with my nose, I peered in. Lark stood in front of the black cloaked one.

Neither moved, and for a moment fear flashed through me that Lark had been hurt or transfixed.

She turned and saw me.

"It's safe. She's taken care of," she said, motioning to the black cloaked one. "Actually, she's playing some kind of game here. Won't talk, won't respond to anything I say."

I sniffed the air, not liking the lack of scent around the

woman. Perhaps it was what she wore that blocked her scent. "I still can't smell her. Can you take that cloak off?"

Lark reached out and grabbed the cloak, only it dissolved as her hand passed through it, as if it never were.

"No, no it can't be," Lark whispered, horror flickering through her and into me—a lightning bolt of emotion.

The girl's mouth was slack and her brown eyes were empty of emotion. Long tendrils of dark brown hair flowed around her face and her features had some similarities with Lark's, though they were subtle. Somehow I didn't think it was because they were both Terralings.

Breath seemed to be coming hard to Lark as she went to her knees. Tears streaked her cheeks and I moved to her side, giving her what comfort I could with my presence. "You used Spirit on her, didn't you?"

"Yes," she said, her voice wavering. "What have I done?"

How did I explain to her that what she'd done was exactly why the Spirit Elementals had been all but wiped out? Though they seemed like they were weak in many respects, they were the deadliest of any of the elements.

A sigh slipped out of me and I settled for a small piece of the truth. "My first charge, he learned to use Spirit, but it is tricky. A powerful tool. When you use it without really knowing, it can burn someone else out."

"Burn them out?" She stared at the girl, her emotions and thoughts racing. "Can it be reversed?"

Hope flared in her and I hated to dash it, but there was no avoiding the truth.

"I don't think so." I pushed my head against her but she pulled away. I understood the need to be alone when a mistake was made. That was something we shared.

We didn't speak as we pushed through the tunnel to the firewyrm's home. There was no room for words.

When we emerged into the large cavern, the children were waiting for us. Tinder saw Lark first before anyone else. His eyes sparkled, the fear of being snatched from his family already fading. A Salamander trait: to live in the moment and forget the past with a speed that left others spinning. Waving wildly, he ran to greet us.

"Terraling, the bad luck cat saved us. I couldn't believe it when I saw her, but she saved us."

I leaned out and gave Tinder's face a lick. "You're welcome, little lizard." At least that had gone right. In itself, it would be enough to win the queen over, of that I was sure.

As a group we worked our way to the entrance where the children were reunited with their families and the queen finally spoke the truth. But we were not done by a long shot.

10

Once the lava flows returned to their natural place, the Salamanders got busy putting their world back as it should be.

We stood with the queen after Lark and Cactus created an oasis and Fiametta softened more than I'd ever seen her.

A soft cough made us all turn to see Jag walking toward us.

She looked away from him and Lark put a hand on her arm. "You should listen to him. The only reason I survived is because I took Peta's advice. Your familiar . . . if he cares for you even half as much as Peta cares for me, you are in good hands."

I had to fight the swell of emotion in me and ended up tucking my head against her neck to hide the pooling tears. "Larkspur, how can you know that?"

She didn't answer me, and she didn't have to; I felt it between us. Our bond was strong, our understanding of each other better than most familiars had after a lifetime of being with their charge. Because of one thing and one thing alone.

Trust.

She trusted me, and in turn I trusted her with my heart and soul. The mother goddess could not have gifted me with a better charge than the half-breed Terraling; even though I *knew* she would push me to the edge of my abilities and then beyond.

From the Pit, we Traveled with Cactus and Ash to the Rim, the home of the Terralings. The smell of the forest was instant, diving into me and striking a chord deep within my bones.

I was home.

Then again, it could have been that I was with Lark. I had a feeling that wherever she was, that would always be home.

Clinging to Lark's shoulders, I was with her as she entered the Spiral, the seat of her father's power.

But it was her older sister, Belladonna who oversaw things in the absence of their father. That he was missing was bad. That he couldn't be found? That was unheard of in the elemental world. Leaders didn't go missing.

I watched as the two sisters spoke, as they clung to each other.

As Belladonna asked Lark to break rules that would have her punished at best, and banished at worst. My heart began to thump so loudly I was sure that Lark would hear it and know the fear that curled through me. To seek out a supernatural for help was a very bad idea, in particular when it was a Tracker. Trackers carried the same blood as Lark, and trouble was bound to double when they were together.

Though it seemed Lark could find enough trouble on her own, I knew it was possible that it could get worse.

She went to one knee and bowed her head. "It will be done."

And with those words I knew I hadn't seen the worst of what could come our way. The only thing I could do was cling to Lark and guide her.

Somehow, I had to believe we would come through this together, and in one piece.

Mother goddess let it be that way. I bowed my head and whispered to myself. "What I can do to save her . . . it will be done."

AFTERWORD

Thank you so much for taking the time to read Peta's side of the story. I hope you enjoyed it! She is one of my favourite sidekicks and I love her to bits, and am so pleased that readers have taken to her as they have. If you want to see more of Peta, continue to read the Elemental series as her role is FAR from over. Happy reading!

www.shannonmayer.com

Made in the USA
Columbia, SC
18 June 2018